D1486860

WHAT CAN WE BE?

Ryan Crawford   Kayla Coombs

First Published 2019

Tiny Tree Children's Books (an imprint of Matthew James Publishing Ltd)

Unit 46, Goyt Mill

Marple

Stockport

SK6 7HX

www.tinytreebooks.com

ISBN: 978-1-910265-85-7

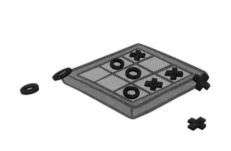

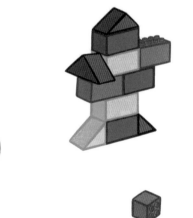

Alone in her room, Millie couldn't stop yawning.
There was nothing to do, it was so very boring.

Her dad said, "Millie, whatever is wrong?"
He could tell she was sad, her face was so long.

"I hate being home," little Millie said.
"I'm so bored I might as well go back to bed."

"Are you sure?" asked her dad. "There's plenty to do."

"When I'm back from work, how about I show you?"

So off went Millie, for a day with her friends,
where there is so much to do and the fun never ends.

Until, of course, they heard the ring of the bell.

"Yay! Home time!" said her best friend Rochelle.

"No fair," said Millie. "Being alone is a BORE."
"I wish we could stay and play some more."

"Really?" said Rochelle. "I can't wait to get home."

"I'll play in my room, but I won't be alone."

"In my room I'm an **astronaut**,
who flies to the stars.
And stops all the aliens
coming from Mars."

"My dad is the **pilot**, he drives our rocket ship."

"To make sure we get back from our outer space trip."

"Wow," said Millie. "In a rocket ship?
Maybe I could come with you, when you take your next trip?
"Don't wait for me!" Rochelle shook her head.
"Why don't you come up with your own game instead?"

"I bet all our friends have their own ways to play.

What will you girls do when you get home today?"

"In my room I'm a **knight**, with a sword and a horse. Who protects the kingdom from dragons of course."

"My dad is the **king**, with a crown made of gold."

"And he claps every time my dragon legends are told."

"In my room I'm a **superhero**,
who flies through the sky.
And protects the city
from the evil bad guy."

"My dad is my **sidekick**, he helps save the day.

We rescue people in our own super way."

"In my room I'm a **pirate**, who nobody can catch
I sail the seas with a hat and eye-patch."

"My dad steers the boat to find all the treasure."

"We can find anything if we're working together."

"In my room I'm a **sorceress**,
I can cast any spell.
And turn naughty people
into frogs as well."

"My dad is a **wizard**, he makes magic too."

"I bet there's an adventure in your room for you."

Millie's friend's stories all sounded so good,
that she rushed to her room as fast as she could.

"Daddy!" said Millie. "Are you ready to play?"
"Of course," said her dad. "I've been waiting all day."

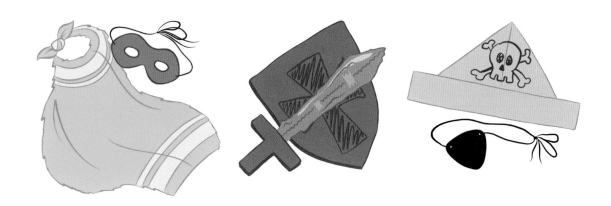

"So tell me, Millie. What can we be?
Heroes? Knights? Pirates?"

"Or maybe all three?"

"Actually," said Millie.
"What would make me so happy."

"Is if we played **firefighters**,
so I can be just like my daddy."

For my Dad, who makes the best pirate hats.
And for Brianna, who would have loved this book.

-Kayla

For my kids.
Whose imagination is my adventure.

-Ryan

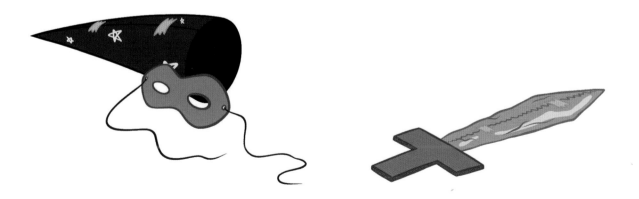